Sandy Creek
387 Park Avenue South
New York, NY 10016

ISBN -13: 978-1-4351-2652-7
Manufactured in China.
Manufactured 09/2011
Lot 11 12 13 SCP 10 9 8 7 6 5 4

I Can Read!™
Picture Book

THE AMAZING SPIDER-MAN

Spider-Man Versus the Vulture

by Susan Hill
pictures by Andie Tong
colors by Jeremy Roberts

Sandy Creek

PETER PARKER

Peter Parker is a very good student.

FLASH THOMPSON

He goes to school with Flash Thompson.

AUNT MAY

Peter lives with his aunt May.

SPIDER-MAN

Peter has a secret identity. He is Spider-Man!

MR. JAMESON

Peter works for Mr. Jameson at the *Daily Bugle*.

THE VULTURE

The Vulture is one of Spider-Man's worst enemies. Can Spidey stop him from causing danger?

Brrrrrring! Class was over. Peter Parker packed up his magnets and grabbed his jacket.

"What's your hurry, Peter?" the teacher asked.

"Today is my first day at the *Daily Bugle*," said Peter.

"I can't be late!"

"Too bad you can't swing on a web like Spider-Man!" said the teacher.

"Ha!" Flash Thompson laughed.

"Peter Parker, a Super Hero? He's just a bookworm!"

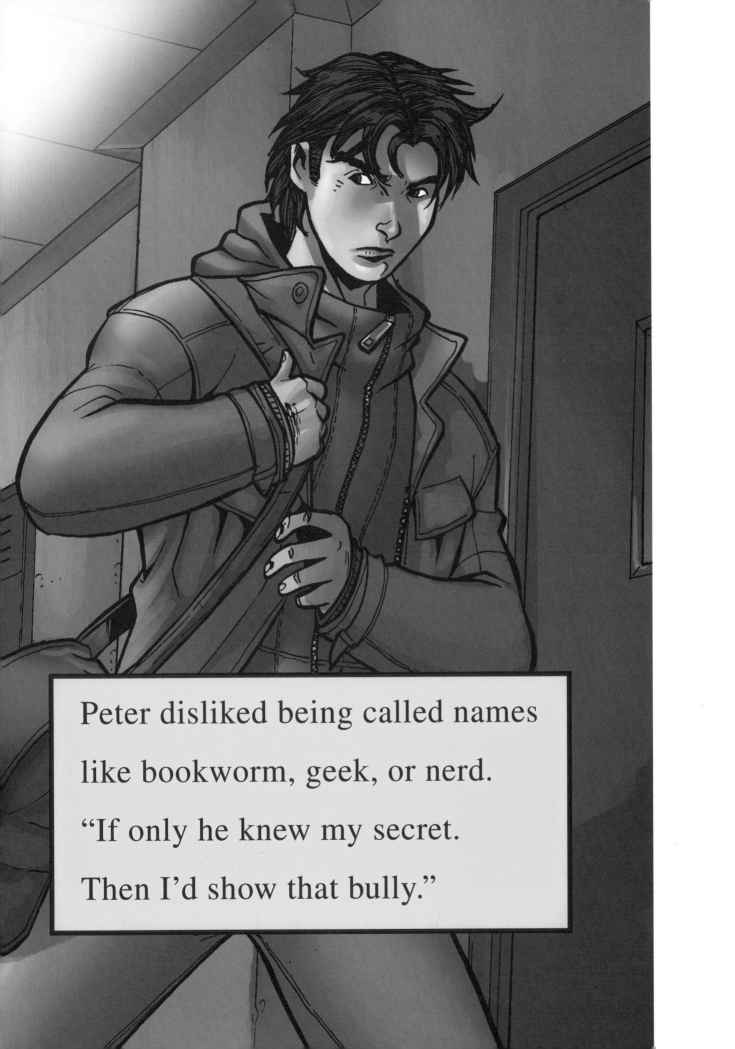

Peter disliked being called names
like bookworm, geek, or nerd.
"If only he knew my secret.
Then I'd show that bully."

Peter was going to be late!

"I know how to get there fast,"

Peter thought.

He ran into an alley

and pulled off his street clothes.

Under Peter's shirt
was a Super Hero costume.
Shy Peter Parker was Spider-Man!

Ever since Peter was bitten

by a super-spider,

he has had superpowers!

He has spider-senses.

He has spider-strength.

And he can climb like a spider!

The Vulture appeared from above.

"What's your hurry, Spider-Man?"

The Vulture was a tricky enemy.

He had wings and could fly.

"Vulture! What are you doing here?"

said Spider-Man.

"I'm stealing this bag of jewels," said the Vulture.

"Just try and stop me!"

"Gosh," Spider-Man thought.

"I am so late.

I must get to the *Daily Bugle*."

Then Spidey remembered something.

With great power comes

great responsibility.

He had to stop the Vulture.

But where had the Vulture gone?

The Vulture swooped behind
Spider-Man on silent wings.
One flick of his wing
sent Spider-Man flying off the roof!

Spider-Man clung to the wall.

"How does Vulture fly

on silent wings?" he thought.

"I know! Silent magnetic power!"

20

Spider-Man climbed up the wall
on a web.

"I'm ready for you this time,
Vulture!" said Spider-Man.

Spider-Man took his homemade

magnet reverser out of his backpack.

"This is the perfect time
to test my invention," he said.
Spider-Man aimed it at the Vulture.

"What did you do?
I can't fly!" said the Vulture.

24

The Vulture crashed to the ground.

"My invention worked!" said Spidey.

The police grabbed the Vulture.

Spider-Man snapped some pictures.

Click-click!

"My new boss will love these photos!"

he said.

Peter put on his street clothes.

He was very late now.

He hurried to the *Daily Bugle*.

The boss, Mr. Jameson, was mad.

"Parker! You're late!" he yelled.

"But wait till you see my photos,"
said Peter.

"How did a shy guy like you
get great photos like these?"
said Mr. Jameson.

"All in a day's work," Peter said.

Mr. Jameson paid Peter well.

Now Peter could do something nice

for his aunt May.

Splash!

"Ha-ha! Sorry, nerd!" said Flash.

"If I used my amazing spider-powers,
he really would be sorry!"
thought Peter.

But Peter was happy,
even if no one could ever know
his amazing secret.

"I'm not a nerd. I'm Spider-Man!"